For Emily, who does the hard work   N.J.

For Paul and Bonnie   C.R.

Sourpuss and Sweetie Pie

Story by **Norton Juster** · Pictures by **Chris Raschka**

MICHAEL DI CAPUA BOOKS **SCHOLASTIC**

Sometimes I'm Sourpuss.

I don't want to be here.
I want to go home and I'm
not coming back, ever.

And sometimes I'm Sweetie Pie.

Can I stay all day, Poppy?
We can play checkers and you
don't even have to let me win.

When I come to Nanna and Poppy's house, Poppy always looks out and says, "Who is it, Sourpuss or Sweetie Pie?"

"Poppy, it's me, let me in."
"I'm not sure," he says.

Poppy doesn't like Sourpuss too much.
Neither does Nanna.
I mean, they like her because she's me,
but not so much. Do you know what I mean?

"Poppy, it's me, Sweetie Pie. I promise."
Then he lets me in.

Most of the time I really am Sweetie Pie.

Look what I brought, Nanna. I made it for you myself.

Tell me the story of how you met Nanna again, Poppy. Especially the part about falling in the water with all your clothes on.

That's my favorite part. Was Nanna as pretty as my mommy?

But sometimes I can be
a real Sourpuss.
Like when I'm angry
or somebody hurts my feelings
or yells at me for no good reason.

Or I can't find any of my stuff
that I really need.

Or I don't want to do
what I'm supposed to do,
especially right now.

I'm not coming out.
I'll stay right here all day.

I don't want you to see me
or look at me, I'm invisible.

You can leave my surprise
on the table.
I won't like it anyway.

I don't know how it's going to be.
It just happens.

I need a hug, Nanna.
The biggest one you've got.

**It's my music and I can play it as loud as I want to—
even louder if I want. Don't you like music?**

Do all Nannas get wrinkles? They look nice on you, Nanna.

**That's all right, Poppy, you can read your book and I'll
read mine here with you. But try not to fall asleep again.**

I don't like orange juice with pieces in it.
The scrambled eggs are runny.
The toast is all burned.
The napkin is on the wrong side,
and it's not my special plate.

When I get big and you get old, Poppy, I'm going to take care of you. You can do whatever you want as long as you clean up when you're done.

I won't wear any of the things you put out for me, Nanna.
I want my yellow shirt with the beads
and the long flowery skirt and
my flip-flops and all my bracelets
or I'm not going to school.
I don't care if it's winter!

You're my best friend, Nanna.
Except for Sara
and Rachel
and Fluffy
and Alphonse
and Consuela.

Oh, and Sally, my goldfish, and Mrs. Whitlock from school.

Let's do a play, Poppy. I'll be Snow White
and you be the prince and the dwarfs
and the wicked queen and everybody else.
Nanna can be the audience. You can make
some popcorn too, and introduce everything.

Will you read me the story again, Poppy? You do the best voices—but don't make it so scary this time.

When I have a bad dream, I'm glad you're right there in the next room, Nanna, and you have a big bed for me to get in with you. But please don't snore.

I don't want to drive anymore. I have to go to
the bathroom again. I feel sick. It's so boring.
I'm going to throw up. Who wants to see
where the Pilgrims landed anyway?
Why can't we stop for a frosty?
Let's go home. NOW!

Sometimes you can go from Sourpuss to Sweetie Pie so quick.

Leave me alone. I don't want to smile, you'll never make me.
Stop making faces, Poppy. I'm only smiling a little bit. I can't help it.

What do you have behind your back? Can I have some?
Not for Sourpuss, for me. I don't know where she went.

I'm Sweetie Pie, can't you tell?

And when it's very late, I can be Sourpuss and Sweetie Pie
all at the same time.

I'm a little tired,
Poppy. Can I
have my bath
and go to bed?

I don't have to go
to bed until I want to
and I'm not dirty
so I'm not going
to take a bath.

Oh, that feels good. Will you do my hair, Nanna? You make it so nice.

You pull it and you twist it and it hurts. Anyway, I don't like curly dark hair. I want long yellow hair.

There's soap in my eyes and nobody likes me at school either.

Will you sing "Hush, Little Baby," Nanna?

Well, maybe I'll listen a little.

And for how long.